Don't Kick Up a Fuss, Gus!

Adria Meserve

little bee books

Gus was a little zebra who lived in Africa. He loved to gallop and jump around on the hot, dusty savanna.

One morning, Gus was playing.
It hadn't rained for ages, so
the ground was very dry.

He stamped his hooves,

he reared,

he bucked . . .

and made the BIGGEST dust clouds ever!

Just then, Mom called Gus. "Come along, dear! We're going on a long walk."

"But I want to make dust clouds," said Gus, digging in his hooves.

"Don't kick up a fuss, Gus!" said Dad. "It's too hot here. The grass is dry and tough, and the river has nearly dried up."

Before Gus could say anything more, his family had trotted off to join the rest of the herd.

They walked along a riverbank and through a forest.

"Walk nose to tail," Mom told Gus.
"No galloping off on your own!" said Dad.

"Walking is boring," moaned Gus. "I want to go home."
Gus's family did their best to make the journey fun.

Dad sang "Five Little Zebras" with Gus,
and Mom sang "Here We Go Round the
Acacia Tree."

When Gus got bored of singing, Grandma played I Spy.
"Are we almost there yet?" asked Gus.

"We're much closer," said Grandpa.
"Let's play Count the Mongooses."

But then they got stuck in a traffic jam.
They waited and waited and waited to cross a bridge.

Gus got really fed up.
"Don't kick up a fuss, Gus!"
Dad said. "There's nothing
we can do."

When they finally reached
the other side of the bridge,
Gus bolted.

He leapt between a giraffe's legs,

over an elephant's trunk, and galloped out of sight.

Gus's family was furious when they
finally caught up to him.
"We're going to finish this walk
even if we have to carry you," said Dad.
"Don't kick up a fuss, Gus!"

But Gus wasn't going to give in just yet.

He kicked up

the biggest

fuss

ever!

Eventually, Gus wore himself out.
"If you're ready now, we'll keep going,"
said Dad. "We need to catch up with the others."

Mom gently pushed Gus along as they
continued on their journey.
"No more fussing," she said.

At last they stopped and rested for the night. "It will all seem better in the morning," said Mom, nuzzling his mane.

The next day, they made better progress.

Gus didn't kick up a fuss—much.

They crossed a river,

trekked up and down a mountain . . .

and finally reached the top of a ridge.

From there they could see a lush, green valley before them.
"We're nearly there!" cried Mom.
Something glistened in the distance.

Gus joined the other zebras as they bounded down the hill, leapt off the grassy bank, and landed in . . .

. . . THE
WATERHOLE!

Gus thought it was wonderful!

Gus jumped and dived
and swooshed down
waterfalls. He made the
biggest waves ever!
"We're all getting wet!"
cried Gus's dad.

Splash!

"Don't kick up a fuss!"
shouted Gus, laughing.

For my lovely Isabelle

little bee books

An imprint of Bonnier Publishing Group
853 Broadway, New York, NY 10003
Copyright © 2009 by Adria Meserve
First published in Great Britain by Piccadilly Press.
This little bee books edition, 2015.
All rights reserved, including the right of reproduction in whole or in part in any form.
LITTLE BEE BOOKS is a trademark of Bonnier Publishing Group,
and associated colophon is a trademark of Bonnier Publishing Group.
Manufactured in China 0215 024
First Edition 2 4 6 8 10 9 7 5 3 1
Library of Congress Control Number: 2014957619
ISBN 978-1-4998-0100-2

www.littlebeebooks.com
www.bonnierpublishing.com